STEVE VOAKE

illustrated by Emma Dodson

This is a work of fiction. Names, characters, places and incidents are either the product of the author's imagination or, if real, used fictitiously. All statements, activities, stunts, descriptions, information and material of any other kind contained herein are included for entertainment purposes only and should not be relied on for accuracy or replicated as they may result in injury.

First published 2011 by Walker Books Ltd
87 Vauxhall Walk, London SE11 5HJ

2 4 6 8 10 9 7 5 3 1

This book has been typeset in StempelSchneidler and EDodson

Printed and bound in Great Britain
by Clays Ltd, St Ives plc

British Library Cataloguing in Publication Data:
a catalogue record for this book is available from the British Library

ISBN 978-1-4063-2240-8

www.walker.co.uk

HOOEY HIGGINS
and the
Big
Boat Race

For Rob, Vivienne and Lucas
S.V.

For Sophie Burdess, with many thanks
E.D.

CONTENTS

Samantha
Hooey
Will
Mr Danson
Twig
Dingbat
Bountiful Bob & the missus
Basbo
Ricky
Wayne

Dad
Mum
Mrs
Jenkins
Miss
Troutson
Grandpa
Grandma

MAGNET MISCHIEF

"Are you sure this is going to work?" asked Twig as Hooey strapped another magnet to his forehead.

"Course it is," said Hooey, picking up an old Coke can. "Loads of pirates must have buried their treasure on the beach and then forgotten about it."

"My dad buried me on the beach once," said Twig as the empty can jumped out of Hooey's hand and clanged against his forehead. "He was halfway home before he remembered."

"There you go then. It's easily done."

"All right, Twig," said Will, checking his notebook. "Today you're going to be flying at a height of approximately four point five centimetres."

"Shweet," said Twig. "Do I get an in-flight meal?"

"Yeah, if you keep your mouth open," said Hooey. "All the sand you can eat."

Strapping the last few magnets to Twig's arms, Hooey stepped back and admired his handiwork. It was surprising what you could achieve with a roll of Sellotape and a box of magnets. Twig now had so many stuck to his body he looked like some kind of weird metallic hedgehog.

"If we find some treasure, can I have a **pirate party**?" he asked as Hooey taped his ears back to lower the wind resistance. "We could dress up and make people walk the plank."

"It's a thought," said Hooey.

"Shame they all died out really. They knew how to have fun, those piratey people."

"I don't think they died out," said Hooey, dusting sand from his fingers. "They probably just got bored of having to fight and look for treasure all the time."

"We played pirate reading games with Mrs Johnson yesterday," said Twig. "I got to sail the high seas looking for connectives."

"Connectives?"

"You know, words like 'and' and 'but'. Basbo said, 'I've found a "but"!' and I laughed and he hit me. But then Samantha came past and said she thought pirates were really cool."

Hooey smiled. "Oh I get it. You just want to have a pirate party so you can invite Samantha."

"I do not," said Twig, blushing beneath the Sellotape. "It just gave me the idea, that's all. Her dad's building her a pirate ship for the boat race."

Hooey frowned.

"What boat race?"

"The first-ever SHRIMPTON-ON-SEA HOME-MADE BOAT RACE," said Twig. "It's in a week's time."

Hooey looked at Will. "We are *so* entering that," he said, grabbing Twig by the ankles. "If we win we might get enough money for Twig's pirate party. Come on. Let's go treasure-hunting."

They ran along the beach, Twig's nose skimming the sand. Every now and then, Hooey checked to see if any treasure had sprung up and stuck itself to Twig's face, but so far there was only a foreign coin and a couple of squashed bottle tops.

"Try waving your arms about," he suggested.

As Twig flapped his arms and made seagull noises, Hooey felt an invisible force start to pull him away. Glancing up, he saw that a large camper van was parked near by.

"Uh-oh," he said.

"EMERGENCY!" shouted Twig, realizing what was about to happen. "BRACE YOUR FACE! BRACE YOUR FACE!" Skidding sideways, he flipped over and whammed into the side of the van.

A tall blond-haired boy of about nineteen jumped out and stared at him in surprise. The magnets had stuck Twig to the passenger door and his arms and legs were splayed out in the shape of a starfish.

"Very artistic," said the boy admiringly. "Can I keep him?"

"Yours for a fiver," said Will. "Plus expenses."

"Will," said Hooey as Twig tried to pull his head away, "I think we should probably get him down."

The older boy grabbed Twig beneath the arms and pulled. "Think I might need some help here," he said as Twig's body clunked back into the van again.

Hooey and Will took hold of a leg each, Hooey shouted "PULL!" and then they all tumbled backwards in a shower of sand.

As Twig sat up and shook sand from his hair, Hooey looked more closely at the older boy. "Hey," he said, "aren't you the twins' brother, Jakey?"

"Yup, that's me, mate," said Jakey. "Just arrived back from New Zealand to set up my own bungee-jumping business. Slight problem though."

"What's that?" asked Hooey.

"I've gone and lost me keys."

Hooey turned to look at Twig, who was still spitting out mouthfuls of sand. "I think we might be able to help you there," he said.

Twig glanced up and saw that everyone was staring at him.

"What?" he asked hopefully. "Have I got treasure on my face?"

"No," said Hooey, "but I think you might have found Jakey's keys."

"Thanks little dude," said Jakey, pulling his keys off Twig's forehead. "Thought I heard you talking about a pirate party earlier on. When's that happening?"

"After we win the boat race," said Twig confidently. "You can come if you like."

"I wouldn't get your hopes up," said Will. "We haven't got any money, or a boat, or enough time to build one."

Hooey smiled.

he said.

SNAP 'N' SQUEAL

The next morning at breakfast, Hooey gave Dingbat the rest of his cereal and watched Grandma Higgins put a large bowl of mush into the microwave.

"What you making, Grandma?" he asked.

"MARITIME MARSHMALLOWS," said Grandma. "Me and Mrs Jenkins are saving up for a new game on the Nintendo Wii, so I thought we'd sell them at next week's boat race. They're my new recipe."

"New recipe?" asked Hooey, moving his toast to the far side of the table. The last time Grandma had used the microwave she had tried to boil an egg and the explosion was so loud that Mrs Wilson from next door had fallen off the toilet and whammed her head on the washbasin. "What's in it?"

"Pancake goo," said Grandma, "all mixed up with marshmallows and sweet candy prawns. You just shove it in the microwave, shut your eyes and hope for the best."

"How long does it take?"

"Oh the microwave decides," said Grandma. "You wait for ages and then all of a sudden it just goes ping and you're done."

"Right," said Hooey. "I think it only goes *ping* because you set the timer, Grandma."

Grandma smiled and patted Hooey's head. "If you say so, dear. If you say so."

* * *

Hooey and Will had almost reached the end of the street when they heard the explosion.

"That was even louder than the last one," said Will. "I hope Mrs Wilson wasn't on the toilet again."

"I hope she was, in a way," said Hooey. "That was a pretty big bang."

When they got to school, Twig was standing in the playground dressed in stripy pyjamas with a towel tucked under his arm.

"Fancy dress, is it?" asked Will.

"Swimming actually," said Twig.

Will frowned. "I thought you were supposed to change when you got there?"

"Well, as they say in the Cubs," replied Twig, "**ALWAYS BE PREPARED**."

"So what exactly does picking up a brick in your pyjamas prepare you for?"

"Being a builder probably. A builder who sleeps in late and gets flooded out."

"Bit random, isn't it?"

"These are random times, Will," said Hooey. "It always pays to be ready."

"Talking of being ready," said Twig, "how's the boat coming along?"

"Still at the planning stage," said Will. "We just need to figure out a way of making it go faster. Maybe you could give it some thought?"

Twig stared at him blankly.

"Or … maybe not," said Will.

* * *

"Now, children," said Miss Troutson as the coach stopped outside the swimming-pool, "what are the three things we need to remember?"

Twig immediately shot his hand up into the air, supporting it with the other hand and shouting, "Ooh, ooh," until Miss Troutson turned to him wearily and raised her eyebrows.

"Yes Twig?"

"Don't Swear, don't break Stuff, and don't Shove

anyone's head down the toilet."

"No," said Miss Troutson, "that's not it. Yasmin?"

"BE SMART, BE SENSIBLE, BE SAFE," said Yasmin.

"Very good, Yasmin," said Miss Troutson. "I'm glad someone's been paying attention."

"I knew that," said Twig sulkily. "I *knew* there were three 'S's!"

"Never mind, Twig," said Hooey. "Yours sounded much more fun."

* * *

While they were waiting for the others to get changed, Hooey and Twig played a game of SNAP 'N' SQUEAL with the Frinton twins. The idea was to pull back the other person's PJs until the elastic was fully stretched, then shout "Snap!" and let go again. If the other person squealed, you scored one point, and if they said a rude word, you got a Sweary Bonus.

Hooey was already three points in front when Basbo stomped out of his cubicle wearing a pair of bright-blue pyjamas. On the front was a picture of a masked wrestler and below it were the words: YOU BIN SLAMMED.

"Is that, like, in a door?" asked Twig. "Because if it is, that's just silly. I slammed my finger in a door once and it really hurt."

Basbo glared at him. "You tryna be funny or summink?"

"No I'm not," said Twig, shaking his head. "I'm just saying that if that man on your pyjamas thinks slamming people's fingers in doors is a good idea, he must be a bit thick."

"Leave it, Twig," said Hooey as Basbo went red in the face. "He's just a wrestler, that's all."

"Yes, and a very silly one," said Twig. "A silly wrestler who should know better than saying stuff on the front of people's pyjamas."

"Bleaarrrgh!" shouted Basbo, charging towards Twig with his fists clenched.

BOUNCING BASBO

"What do you mean: he's stuck in a locker?" asked Miss Troutson.

"I don't really know how else to explain it," said Hooey. "He just sort of got folded in there."

"That's ridiculous," said Miss Troutson. "People don't get folded into lockers."

Hooey followed Miss Troutson back into the changing rooms, where Ricky Mears was doing a dance along the benches in his underpants. When he saw Miss Troutson, he screamed, slipped over and fell into the waste bin.

"You silly boy," said Miss Troutson, shaking Ricky out onto the floor. "What did I say about being sensible and safe?"

"I was being sensible!" cried a muffled voice from the direction of the lockers. "I was being safe!"

"Number twenty-nine, I think," said Hooey helpfully.

Miss Troutson went over to locker number twenty-nine and turned the key. The door swung open to reveal Twig inside with his legs around his head.

"Why hel-*lo* Miss Troutson," he said politely as if she had just popped round for a cup of tea. "This *is* a nice surprise."

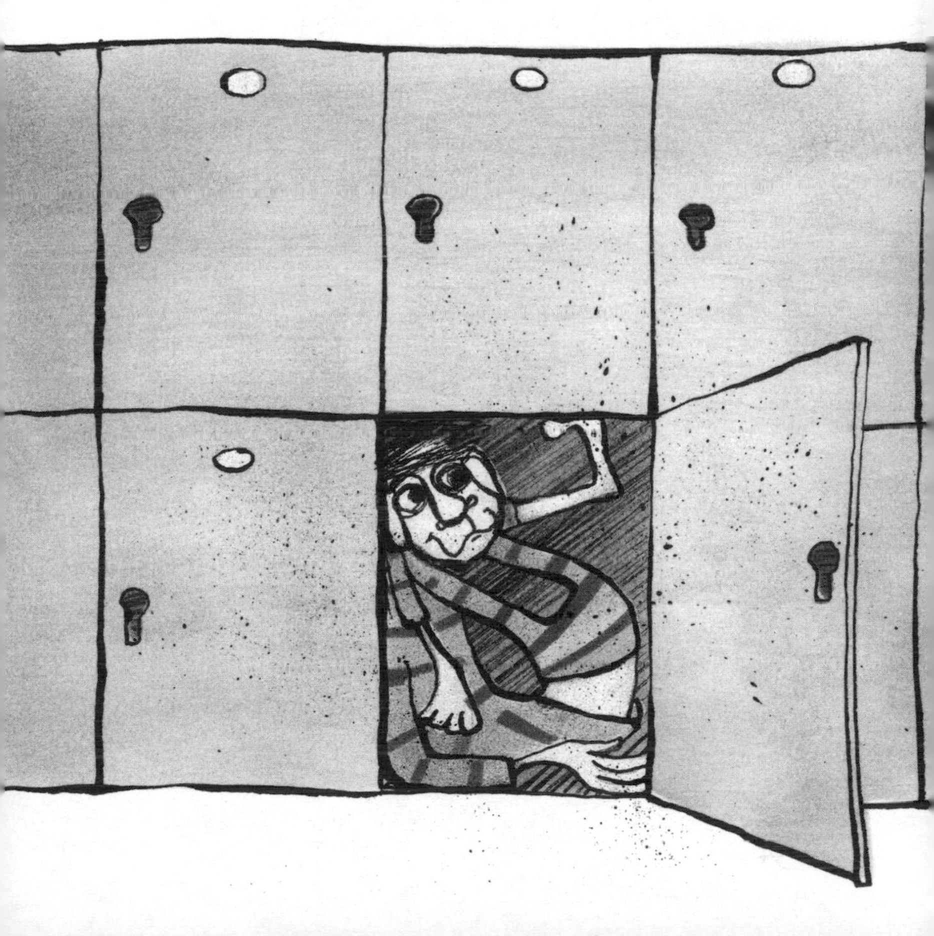

"GOOD GRIEF, CHILD!" cried Miss Troutson, stepping back in amazement. "How on earth did you get in there?"

"Well a funny thing happened," said Twig as Basbo raised his fist behind Miss Troutson's back. "I remembered Mr Croft telling us in assembly that anything is possible. And I thought, I wonder if it's possible for me to get into this locker? And now I'm thinking, I wonder if it's possible for me to get out again?" He paused and looked at Miss Troutson. "What do you think?"

"I think," said Miss Troutson, "that if you're not out of there in the next five seconds, you're going to be spending the rest of your swimming lessons in the headteacher's office."

"Ooh," said Twig excitedly. "Has he got his own pool?"

Miss Troutson turned and pointed at Basbo. "You. Come and give me a hand."

Basbo grinned so that Hooey could see the gaps between his teeth. "I grabbim an pullimout an frowim frewawallannat," he said.

"Thank you Barry," said Miss Troutson. "That's very helpful of you."

"Don't worry," said Twig, squirming around inside the locker. "I'm sure I can manage."

"Nonsense," said Miss Troutson. "Just you hold still and we'll have you out of there in no time. All right, Barry? You take that leg and I'll take this one."

"Grabbawldavvimmm!" said Basbo, seizing Twig's right leg.

"Here goes!" cried Miss Troutson, grabbing hold of Twig's left leg.

"ONE ..."

"Can I just ..."

"... TWO ..."

"Maybe if I ..."

"... THREE ..."

"I really don't think ..."

"... PULL!"

Miss Troutson and Basbo leaned back at the same time, pulling so hard that the veins stood out on their foreheads. The lockers creaked. Twig groaned. Then, just when it seemed as if Twig's legs were about to separate from the rest of his body, he flew out of the locker, sailed across the benches and smacked head first into the lockers on the other side of the room.

There was a loud
FTAANNGGG!

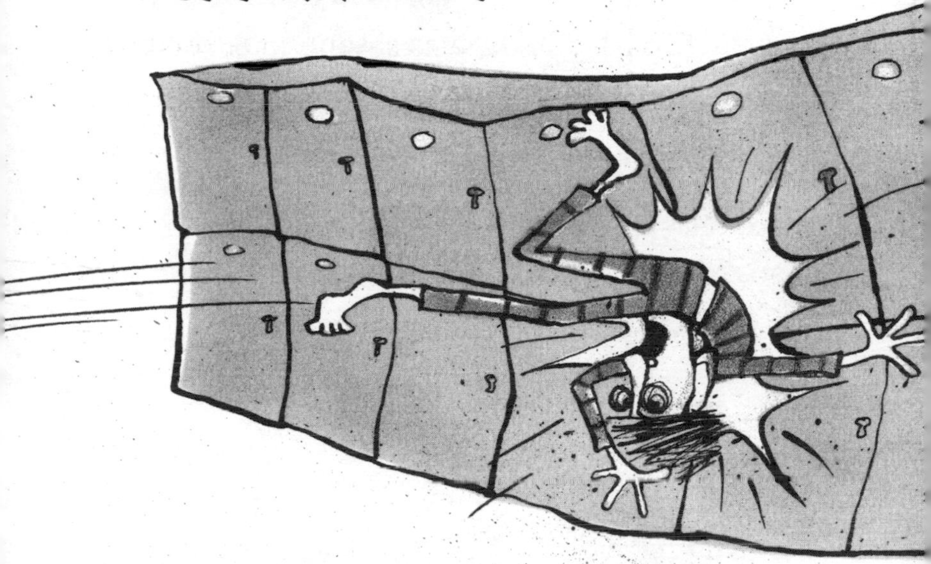

and then all the boys
clapped and cheered as Twig slid down
onto the floor, the sound of clanging metal
echoing around the changing room.

"Ow," Twig said, holding his head.
"I think I broke my brain."

Hooey smiled.

"No harm done then," he said.

* * *

"But Barry, you *have* to get your pyjamas wet," Miss Troutson was saying to Basbo on the far side of the pool. "That's the whole point of wearing them."

"No pyjamas wet!" growled Basbo, shaking his head. "Dry-clean only. Dry. Clean. Only!"

"Now come on, Barry. Don't be si—"

"DRY-CLEAN-ONLY-DRY-CLEAN-ONLY-DRY-CLEAN-ONLY!" said Basbo, putting his fingers in his ears.

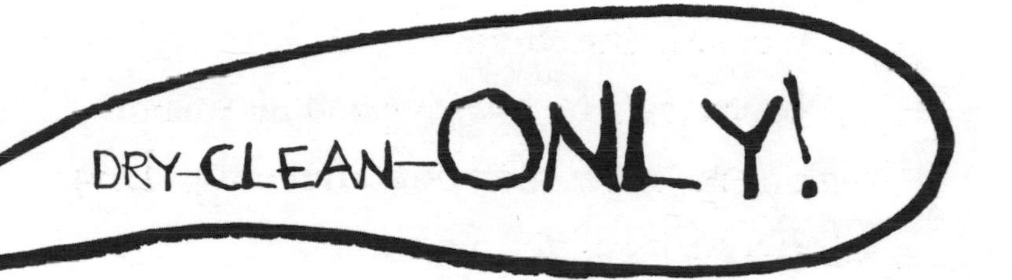

"Right," said Miss Troutson. "Well, if you're going to be silly about it, you'll just have to stay where you are."

Basbo watched her go, then took his fingers out of his ears and stared into the pool.

"Dry-clean only," he said quietly.

"Now then," said Miss Troutson, lining everyone else up on the other side of the pool. "Make sure you all listen carefully to what Mrs Cole has to say."

Hooey stared at the muscular figure of Mrs Cole as she stood glowering, her arms folded, at the end of the pool and wondered a) if there was a Mr Cole and b) if he ever wished his life had turned out differently.

He put his hand up.

"Yes Hooey?"

"Umm, Miss Troutson, where's Miss Wickham?"

"Following last term's incident with the bubble bath," replied Miss Troutson icily, "Miss Wickham has decided on a change of career."

Hooey noticed Frank and Freddie Frinton smirking and remembered how they'd shaken two family-sized bottles of FOAM & AWAY into the water when no one else was looking. By the time everyone had swum a couple of lengths, the bubbles were nearly up to the ceiling and all you could hear was the sound of people calling, "Hello? Is anyone there?" and the crack of heads as they swam into one another.

Later that week the class had done a piece of writing called "The Happiest Day of My Life" and almost everyone had written about it except for Basbo, who wrote about his garage exploding, and Sarah-Jane Silverton, who wrote about fluffy kittens. But the downside of it all was that the smiling face of Miss Wickham had now been replaced by someone who looked as though she had eaten a wasps' nest for breakfast.

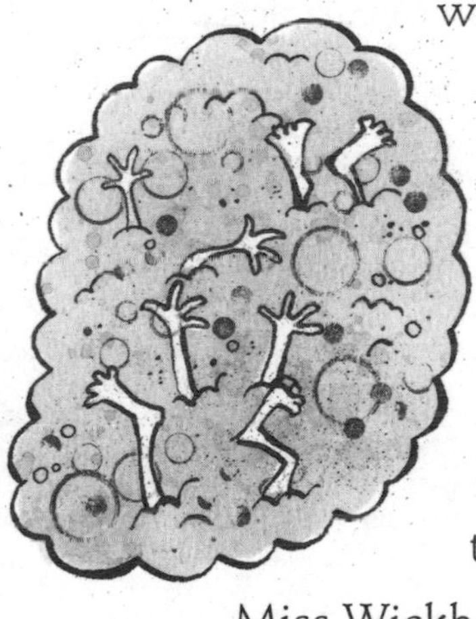

"You," she said, pointing at Twig.

"Me?" said Twig, pointing at himself.

"Yes you. Come here boy."

Twig grinned happily. "I've been picked," he whispered as he scampered along the side of the pool. "I've been pickety-picked!"

Mrs Cole looked at him doubtfully. "Can you swim?" she asked.

"Yes," said Twig. "Plus I can get four gobstoppers in my mouth and I can do dog impressions."

"Stop talking," said Mrs Cole, holding up her hand. "Just stop talking and get in the pool."

"Whatever you say," said Twig. "You're the boss."

With that he leapt into the air, clasped his knees together and hit the water with a loud

BU-DOOOF!

A curtain of water sprayed upwards and outwards, drenching Mrs Cole on one side of the pool and Basbo on the other. For a few seconds Basbo stared at Twig, water dripping from the end of his nose. He looked down at his pyjamas. Then he looked back at Twig again. Twig smiled weakly at him from the middle of the pool.

"Now then Barry," said Miss Troutson as Basbo started to growl, "I'm sure Twig didn't mean to get water on your jim-jams."

muttered Basbo, taking several steps backwards.

"Dry-CLEAN-ONLY!"

With an angry shout he ran as fast as he could towards the edge of the pool, intending to land on Twig's head from a very great height. But as he jumped, his foot slipped and instead of hitting Twig he landed feet first on a large blue float.

Perhaps if he hadn't been travelling so fast, or if he'd hit the float at a slightly different angle, the results wouldn't have been quite so spectacular. As it was, Basbo skimmed across the surface at such speed that he

carved a deep groove in the water, bouncing at least four times before he hit the side of the pool and took off into the air.

For a moment time seemed to slow down, as if it didn't want anyone to miss either the bewildered look on Basbo's face or the horrified look on Mrs Cole's. Then suddenly it went back to normal again and Basbo arrived in her arms at approximately one hundred miles an hour, blasting her off her feet and backwards into the baby-pool.

As the rest of the class cheered and ran over to watch Miss Troutson try and free them both from beneath the hippo slide, Hooey stayed where he was, staring into the pool with a big smile on his face.

"Of course," he whispered.

Just wait until Will hears about this!

TOMMY'S TAKEAWAY

"Good work, Hooey," said Will as they sat on the grass looking out across the river. "I think you might be on to something there."

"I don't get it," said Twig. "What's Basbo's accident got to do with anything?"

"BOUNCING BOMBS," said Hooey.

"Huh?" said Twig.

"BOUNCING BOMBS," repeated Hooey. "Grandpa said they used to drop them on the water during the war and they bounced until they reached their target. Which, in our case, will be the finishing line."

"In *our* case?"

"That's right," said Will, unrolling a sheet of wallpaper. He pointed to a diagram of a raft with a giant catapult behind it. "While everyone else is paddling, we'll be bouncing. And *flying*."

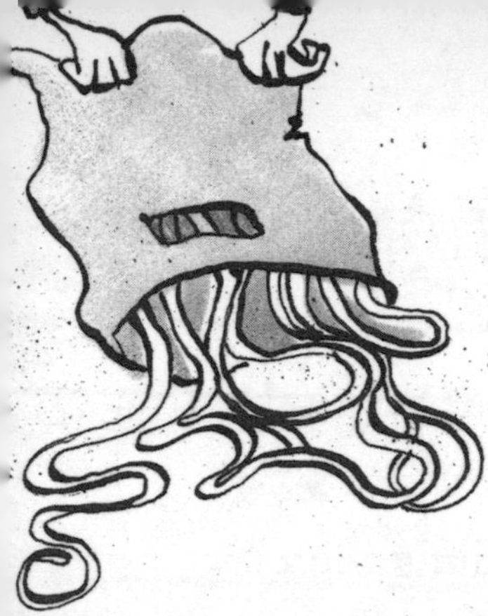

He picked up two large carrier bags and shook them out onto the grass.

Aaagh,

screamed Twig. "Snakes!"

"Relax," said Hooey. "They're elastic ropes. We found them in the garage with the camping stuff." He stretched one out to demonstrate. "See?"

"I knew that," said Twig, coming out from behind a tree. "I so knew that."

"Anyway," said Will, "when the race starts we'll fire ourselves off the bank, bounce up the river and pass the other boats at approximately—" he flipped through his notebook— "ninety-four miles an hour."

"Isn't that a bit dangerous?" asked Twig.

"Goldie the goldfish was only doing about twenty and he got killed."

Hooey frowned. "Goldfish can't swim that fast, Twig."

"Goldie wasn't swimming," said Twig sadly. "I was cleaning out his little fish tank so I scooped him up in one of those nets. It got caught on the side and when I tried to pull it free he went flying across the room." Twig shook his head. "My mum said it was just nature's way. But I've seen loads of wildlife programmes on the Discovery Channel and they've never shown a fish getting wanged against a window."

Hooey patted his arm. "Don't upset yourself, Twig. No one's going to get wanged against anything. And besides, Will's designed a special braking system, haven't you Will?"

"Sure have."

Will picked up a rucksack and pulled out a pink duvet cover with pictures of angels on it. The words *Sweet Dreams* were picked out in yellow stitching.

"Bit girly," said Twig. "I'm not sleeping in that."

"It's not for sleeping in," replied Hooey, showing Twig how the corners were attached to the top of the rucksack with bits of string. "It's a parachute. It stays packed away until we reach the finishing line and then **FLUMP** it opens up and slows us down."

"How does it know when to open?"

"It doesn't know, Twig. We have to *make* it open."

Twig frowned. "You can't make duvet covers do stuff, Hooey. They're not like little kids or anything."

Hooey held up a ball of string for Twig to look at. "String, yes?"

"String," agreed Twig.

"Parachute?" said Hooey, pointing to the middle of the duvet cover.

"Parachute."

"OK. At the start of the race, we tie one end of the string to a tree and the other end to the parachute. When we get to the end, it pulls the parachute open."

"But how does the string *know*?"

"How does the string know what?"

"How does the string know when to open the parachute?"

Hooey looked at Will and sighed. "Because it's clever string, Twig, OK? It's *clever* string."

"Wow," said Twig, putting his hands up to his cheeks. "The things they can do nowadays!"

"That's still not enough," said Will as Twig reached in and pulled another empty plastic milk carton from the recycling skip. They were standing in the supermarket car park, but it was still early and there was no one else around.

Hooey stared at the wheelbarrow full of empty cartons and scratched his head. "Are you sure we need more?" he asked.

"We're going to need hundreds," said Will.

Twig stuck his head through the metal flap and peered into the skip. "There are loads in here. Maybe we could just suck 'em out with a Hoover."

"Or maybe we could hold your ankles and lower you in."

"What?" said Twig. "Why me?"

"'Cos you're the only one thin enough."

"But what if I fall in? I might never be found again."

"It's not the Amazon, Twig. It's Sainsbury's car park."

"OK," said Twig. "But I'm going to need a secret code in case any spies are listening."

"Spies?" said Will. "Why would there be spies in Sainsbury's car park?"

"Because," said Twig, tapping the side of his nose, "that's where you'd least expect them."

Will sighed. "OK, Twig, what's the code?"

"The code is … if everything's going well and I get the stuff, I'll shout, Carton contact! Take out the Twig! Then what happens is: you take me out. See how it works?"

"Yeah, I think we get that," said Hooey. "Anything else?"

"Yes," said Twig, "and this is particularly important. If there's no oxygen, or I'm attacked by giant rats or zombies or something, I'll shout—" Twig looked at the row of shops across the street— "I'll shout, Tommy's Takeaway! Tommy's Takeaway! and then you have to pull me up really fast."

"Twig, it's a recycling bin. There won't be any zombies in there."

Twig narrowed his eyes. "That's what they *want* you to think."

"Fine. Tommy's Takeaway it is. Now can we please get on with it?"

Twig stuck his head hesitantly through the flap, like a cat on a rainy day.

"How's it looking?" asked Hooey. "Any rats? Zombies?"

"Not so far," said Twig, his voice echoing around the container. "They're probably hiding."

When their arms were at full stretch and only Twig's trainers were showing, Twig shouted, "Carton contact! Take out the Twig!" and they hauled him up again.

"Ker-*ching*," said Twig, dropping four empty cartons into the wheelbarrow.

"Mission accomplished."

"Not quite," said Will. "We need another twenty."

"Twenty?"

"Don't think about it, Twig," said Hooey. "Just think about bouncing over the finishing line at ninety miles an hour."

"Ninety-four," said Will.

"We'd better hurry up," said Hooey as a lorry rumbled into the car park. "People are starting to arrive."

As they fed Twig through the slot again, Hooey's hands suddenly felt very light. When he looked down, he saw that he was holding an empty trainer.

"Uh-oh," said Will, who was holding the other one. "I think we lost him."

shouted an echoey voice.

"Don't panic, Twig," said Hooey. "We'll go and get some rescue equipment. Won't be a minute."

"But what about the rats and zombies?"

"If you see any, just wop 'em over the head with a milk carton," said Hooey. "They hate that apparently."

* * *

When Hooey and Will arrived back at the skip with a rope and some biscuits, Hooey posted a custard cream through the slot then banged on the side of the container. "Twig, can you hear me?"

"Maybe he's sulking," said Will when there was no reply. "Give me a leg up and I'll take a look."

Hooey linked his hands together and Will climbed up and peered in through the flap.

"I don't want to worry you," he said, "but I think he's disappeared. Maybe the zombies got him after all."

"Or…" said Hooey.

"Or what?"

"Or *that*," said Hooey as they both turned and watched a big lorry lumbering out of the car park. On the back was a large metal container with the words

KEEPING BRITAIN GREEN on the side of it.

Hooey looked at Will. "Are you thinking what I'm thinking?" he asked.

"I think I am," said Will.

By the time they got to the entrance, the lorry had already turned left and was rumbling away down the street. All they could hear was the rattle of the engine and a thin, reedy voice shouting "TOMMY'S TAKEAWAY! TOMMY'S TAKEAWAY!"

"I don't know about you," said Hooey, "but I did *not* see that one coming."

PLANKS AND PLANS

"It was all right once I got there," said Twig as the three of them sat by the river. "And when the people at the recycling centre stopped laughing, they gave me all these plastic cartons."

"Nice work, Twig," said Hooey. "Now all we've got to do is fix these planks together, tie the cartons underneath and set up the catapult."

"Piece of cake," said Will. "Take about ten minutes, I reckon."

* * *

Five hours later, Hooey helped Will stretch the elastic ropes back between two trees before tying them to a third one. Hooey pushed the raft until it was resting against the giant catapult, then handed Twig a large pair of scissors.

"There you go," he said. "You're **Chief Cutter**."

"Brilliant!" said Twig proudly as they clambered onto the raft.

He thought for a moment. "What's a **Chief Cutter**?"

"The person who cuts the rope."

"Gotcha."

Hooey gripped one of the drawer handles that Will had screwed to the side of the raft, then turned to Twig and put his thumb up. "OK, Twig," he said, "let's see what this bad boy can do."

As Twig began snipping through the rope, Hooey gritted his teeth and stared out across the water.

This was it.

The big test run was finally here.

He shut his eyes. Any second now…

There was a soft TWANG, then the raft slithered slowly across the grass, slid down the bank and came to rest at the edge of the river.

Hooey opened his eyes and looked at Will. "Is it me," he said, "or were we supposed to go faster than that?"

Will unrolled his plans and sucked air through his teeth. "I don't think those ropes have got enough **wallop** in them," he said. "What are we going to do? There's no way we can win this race now."

"Positive thinking," said Twig. "That's what we need. I didn't think I could get folded into that locker, but I managed it. Like Mr Croft said: anything's possible if you put your mind to it."

Will looked at him.

"Well OK, maybe not *my* mind. But yours, definitely. That magnety thing was brilliant."

"Yeah, so brilliant we didn't find a single piece of treasure," said Will glumly.

"We found Jakey's keys though," said Hooey. "So it was still a result."

"Maybe that's the secret," said Twig. "Maybe you have to come up with stuff by accident."

"Twig's right," said Hooey. "Basbo's crash

at the swimming-pool was an accident, but it gave us the idea for the bouncing boat. And finding Jakey's keys was an accident, but I think it's just given us the answer to our problems."

"Has it?" said Will. "How?"

"Ooh I know," said Twig excitedly. "We could tie floats round Jakey's van, drive it across the water and then everybody would go Oh no! and we'd win the race!"

Will raised his eyebrows and looked at Hooey.

"Or," said Hooey, "we could just borrow his bungee rope."

"I was going to say that," said Twig. "It was going to be my next suggestion."

"I can hear voices," said Will as they walked back along the footpath towards the gate. Hooey listened and, sure enough, he could hear a deep, rasping growl that reminded him of sandpaper on metal.

"Basbo," he whispered.

Through a gap in the trees they could see Basbo standing by the river with several planks of wood arranged around him in the shape of a boat. Ricky Mears and Wayne Burkett were kneeling beside him, nailing the planks together.

"There's no way that's gonna float," said Twig as he watched Ricky and Wayne pull on masks and snorkels before stepping inside the boat with Basbo. "They haven't got milk cartons or anything."

As Basbo, Ricky and Wayne picked the boat up by the sides and began walking into the river, Hooey realized that it didn't even have a bottom.

"Twig," he said, shaking his head in amazement as their heads disappeared beneath the surface, "it's official. There are actually people in this world who are even dafter than you are."

"Really?" said Twig.

MARITIME MARSHMALLOWS

Hooey woke up early and looked out of the window. The sun was shining, the birds were singing and Grandpa was in the garden with Alfie Rossiter. Next to them was a large grey object with HMS HIGGINROSS written on the side of it. Either there had been an unusually high tide, or Grandpa and Alfie had gone and built themselves a battleship.

"WOAH!" shouted Hooey.

Will opened one eye and peered out from the lower bunk.

"What's up?" he asked. "Aliens on the roof again?"

"Better than that," said Hooey. "There's a battleship on our lawn."

* * *

"What do you think of her then, boys?" asked Grandpa, nailing a wooden anchor to the side. "She's a beaut, ain't she?"

"Very impressive," said Will.

"Runs on manpower," said Alfie. "Or rather, womanpower."

"*Woman*power?"

"You'd better believe it," said Grandpa. "Grandma and Mrs Jenkins were playing Pro Wrestling on the Nintendo Wii and they found the body slams a bit tiring. So I told 'em if they did some rowing for us, they'd soon be fighting fit!"

At that moment, Grandma and Mrs Jenkins came jogging out onto the lawn. Mrs Jenkins was wearing a pink bodysuit with matching gloves and a pair of wrestling boots laced up to her knees. Grandma was dressed in a lemon-yellow tracksuit with orange trainers and a pair of Grandpa's old motorcycling gloves.

"RUNNING ON THE SPOT, VERA!" Grandma called, coming to a halt beside the rhododendrons. "LET'S GET THOSE KNEES UP!"

They began pumping their legs up and down until they were a blur of lemony pink and their knees were nearly touching their noses.

"Steady, girls," said Grandpa. "You don't want to wear yourselves out before the race starts."

"No chance of that!" said Mrs Jenkins. "We've had some **Maritime Marshmallows** and we're ready to rumble!"

"Sugar high," Will whispered. *"Don't get too close."*

"Come on, Vera," cried Grandma, elbowing Mrs Jenkins in the ribs, "let's run the little boat down to the river!"

"Little boat?" said Alfie Rossiter, a horrified look on his face. "Little *boat*?"

"Easy now, love," said Grandpa as Grandma strained to lift one end of the ship onto her back. "Alfie and I are going to pop it on the back of the trailer."

"What?" cried Mrs Jenkins, who was already trying to lift up the other end.

"WHAT, WHAT, WHAT?"

"They're saying they don't need us," said Grandma.

"Won't feed us?" cried Mrs Jenkins, clasping her hands dramatically to her chest. "Then I shall simply die of hunger!"

"Have another Maritime Marshmallow," said Grandma, stuffing one in her mouth for her.

"Ulp," said Mrs Jenkins through a mouthful of marshmallow. "Thamp-thoo."

* * *

When they got to the river, Mr Maplewick the Mayor was walking up and down the bank, shouting advice through a megaphone.

"PLENTY OF ROOM FOR EVERYONE!" he called. "ALL BOATS TO THE STARTING LINE!"

Jakey Frinton had already fixed the bungee rope between the two trees, using his camper van to stretch it back as far as it would go then tying it to another tree.

"Wow," said Twig as they sat on the raft. "We are *so* gonna die."

A group of firemen paddled onto the river in a big yellow helmet. "Back up a bit, chaps!" shouted the mayor. "Back behind the starting line."

Hooey watched as Bob from **BOB'S BOUNTIFUL BAKERY** helped his wife into a huge inflatable doughnut. Behind him, the ladies from Shrimpton Women's Institute paddled around in a glass boat made entirely from jam jars. They were tied together with a special waterproof wool that Gladys Gladdison had developed during a wet camping holiday in Rhyl. While the other ladies used gardening spades to splash up and down the river, Gladys sat on a cushion calling out, "Left a bit, girls!" or "Steady as she goes!" before pencilling another answer into the Saturday crossword.

"You gonna be OK now, little dudes?" asked Jakey. "Think I'm gonna go and have me a lie-down."

"Thanks Jakey," said Twig. "See you at my pirate party."

"Not if we don't get a move on, you won't," said Will. "The race is about to start."

Down on the river, Mr Danson was bobbing around in a hollowed-out log he had painted pink to look like a stick of rock. Next to him, Philbert the Farmer was sitting with Philbert Junior on some sacks of straw wrapped up in black plastic with white patches stuck all over it. They had glued a selection of vegetables together to make a head so that, from a distance, it looked as though they were riding an enormous cow.

"Wouldn't fancy milking that," said Hooey.

"Nor me," said Twig. "That is one scary bit of dairy."

Just behind Philbert and Philbert, Frank and Freddie Frinton were pushing a Lilo towards the starting line. Hooey noticed that Jakey was fast asleep on it, snoring gently and clutching a half-eaten bag of crisps in one hand.

"I didn't know he was taking part," said Twig as Frank and Freddie giggled their way back up the bank.

"I don't think he did either," said Hooey. "Come on, let's get going."

They backed the raft up against the bungee rope and Hooey heard the trees creaking under the strain.

"By my calculations," said Will, checking his plans, "this bungee rope is at least a thousand times more powerful than the other one. So with any luck we'll hit three hundred and seventeen miles an hour before we run out of river."

"Three hundred and s—" squeaked Twig. "Why do you w—"

"Water-speed record," said Will, opening his notebook and tapping it with his finger. "Last set in 1978." He held up a metal rod with a bicycle wheel on the bottom and an old car speedometer on the top. "The speedo only goes up to a hundred and ten, so as long as it spins round three times, we'll know we've beaten it."

"Genius," said Hooey. "Twig, parachute?"

Twig patted the rucksack on his back.

"Look," said Will, "there's Grandpa."

Hooey turned to see Grandpa's battleship sailing up to the starting line. Alfie was checking out the competition through a telescope while Grandpa relaxed in one of the deckchairs, waving to the crowds who had gathered along the bank. On either side of the ship were Grandma and Mrs Jenkins, paddling away with a couple of shovels from the allotment.

As Hooey watched, Grandma gave two quick blasts on the air horns attached to her hat and shouted:

Hooey nodded. "She did."

A man in safari shorts threw fifty pence onto the deck and with a cry of "Customer contribution!" Grandma loaded a large

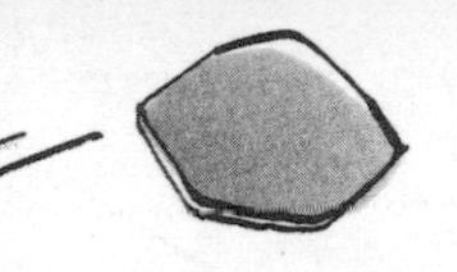

Maritime Marshmallow into a catapult, pulled back the elastic and let it fly. The marshmallow exploded across the man's face with a **THWACK** but to Hoocy's surprise he licked his lips and put his thumbs up.

"Dee-licious!" he declared. "Marshmallow-tastic!"

The crowd roared and soon Grandma was so busy firing off snacks that she forgot to paddle and the ship began to turn round in circles.

"Engine failure! Engine failure!" shouted Alfie.

"**Yowzer!**" cried Grandma, swapping her catapult for the shovel. "More mallows later, darlings! More mallows later!"

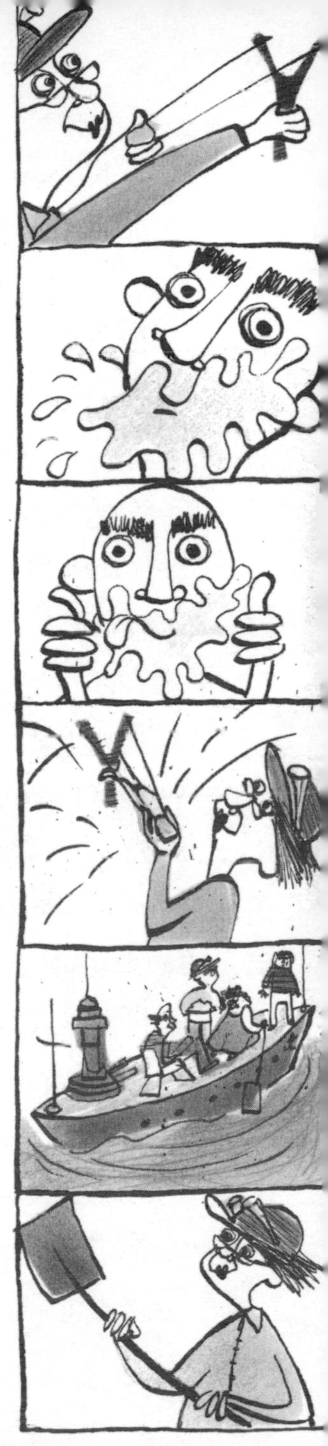

"OK Twig," said Hooey as everyone paddled towards the starting line, "get ready with the scissors."

Twig looked at him. "What scissors?"

"The ones you were supposed to bring to cut through the rope."

"Oh," said Twig, "*those* scissors." He smiled weakly.

"Twig!"

"Maybe we could borrow their knife," said Will, pointing to Bob and his wife, who were sitting in the middle of their inflatable doughnut. A selection of bread rolls and sugary buns was spread out across their laps and Bob was poised with a nutty roll in one hand and a sharp knife in the other.

"Excuse me," called Will, "we were just wondering if we could borr—" But before he could finish, Dingbat gave a hungry yelp, launched himself off the top of the bank and landed in Bob's lap.

"DO NOT OVERLOAD THE VEHICLES!" the mayor shouted sternly through his megaphone. "DO NOT OVERLOAD THE V—"

At which point Dingbat opened his mouth, bit down hard and the inflatable doughnut exploded with a loud…

BANG!

"They're off!" cried a small boy.

"HOORAY!" shouted the crowd.

"Eh?" said the mayor, staring at his starting pistol. Then he threw it over his shoulder and shouted,

Hooey watched Twig attempt to gnaw through the rope as the rest of the boats paddled away up the river. "I don't think that'll do it, Twig," he said.

At that moment, something stirred beneath the surface of the water and Hooey saw that something shadowy was moving along the river bed.

"Will," he said, "am I dreaming?"

"Don't think so," said Will. "Why?"

"Because I've just seen Basbo and his mates at the bottom of the river. And I think they were in a submarine."

PERISCOPE PERIL

Further down the river, things were really hotting up. The ladies from the Women's Institute had got off to a flying start, flailing their gardening spades so fast that their arms were a blur of coloured cardigans. Gladys Gladdison had thrown her crossword away and was jumping up and down shouting,

"WIN OR DIE
WIN OR DIE
WIN OR DIE – IT'S THE WI!"

Up on the bank the firemen's friends and family were chanting,

"NEE-NAW, NEE-NAW.
WHAT'S THAT NOISE?
NEE-NAW, NEE...
IT'S THE FIREMAN BOYS!"

And beside them Philbert the Farmer's wife was banging two saucepans together, yelling,

"HEY! WOW! A GURT BIG COW! THERE'S NO WAY YOU'RE GONNA WIN NOW!"

The noise was incredible.

It was madness and chaos all rolled into one.

And in the midst of this mad, noisy chaos, Basbo, Ricky and Wayne ran silently along the river bed in their bottomless boat. All of them were wearing masks, all of them were breathing through long metal tubes, and all of them were definitely up to no good.

On the surface, Derek Danson was edging ahead of the firemen and playing little snatches of sea shanties on the mouth organ his mother had given him for his birthday. "Any requests?" he called to the ladies of the WI.

"Yes," replied Gladys. "Get out of the way so we can win."

"Don't know that one," said Derek. "How about A Life on the Ocean Wave?"

He was about to start improvising when there was a scraping noise below and he looked down to see a drill poking through the bottom of his boat. The drill disappeared before popping up again further along. Soon there were several holes in the bottom of the boat and Derek Danson was swooshing around in a rising puddle of water.

"CODE RED!" he cried, dropping his mouth organ.

Back at the starting line, Hooey watched Mr Danson's boat sinking and saw the race leaders pulling ahead. It was all happening on the river, but they were still stuck on the bank, going nowhere.

Suddenly, Bob the Baker popped his head out of the water, a soggy doughnut stuck to the side of his face.

"Here you go lads," he said, waving his knife. "It's too late for me and the missus, but I reckon you can still make it."

"Thanks Mr Babbington!" said Hooey as Dingbat scrambled out of the water with four doughnuts in his mouth. He handed Twig the knife. "Looks like we're on our way, Twiggy-boy!"

Hooey held on tightly to the raft's handles as Twig sawed through the rope.

“Guess we’d better hang on, eh Will?”

At least, that was what he’d meant to say. But he only got as far as “Guess we’d better ha—” before the rope snapped and flung the raft forward so fast that Hooey thought his head was going to come off.

"WAAAAAAAH!" cried Twig, hanging off the back as the raft flew across the water, skimming the surface and sending waves splashing into the bank. As the crowd became a blur, Hooey's cheeks flapped in the wind and his eyes watered so much he could barely make out the shapes of the boats as they shot past. They overtook Mr Danson, zoomed past the firemen and then, just as they were about to pass the ladies from the WI, the front of the raft tipped forwards, dug itself into the water and Hooey suddenly found himself flying very fast

through the air. As he sped past a seagull he noticed that Will was cruising alongside him, still staring at his plans and trying to figure out what had gone wrong. Dingbat was running behind in midair, his mouth full of doughnuts and his ears streaming in the breeze. Hooey looked up and saw that Twig was high above them all, a tiny dot in a big blue sky.

Far below, the crowd stared up with their mouths wide open in surprise.

Hooey was just wondering whether he would carry on flying for ever when he noticed that he had stopped travelling forwards and was travelling downwards instead. Then he hit the water with a mighty

KER-SPLOSH!

and opened his eyes to see Basbo, Ricky and Wayne trundling along the bottom of the river in their home-made submarine, searching for their next victim.

As Will landed next to him, Hooey waved and then they were pulled out of the water by Grandpa and Alfie.

"Hooey, m'boy," said Grandpa as Dingbat scrabbled aboard behind them, "what happened to your raft?"

"Hit the water and exploded," said Will.

"So annoying when they do that," said Alfie, at which point Twig landed on his head. They crashed down onto the deck and the duvet parachute covered them both with a FLUUUMP.

Twig stuck his head out, looking confused. He glanced down at the duvet cover. Then he smiled, kissed Alfie on the cheek and put his thumb in his mouth. "Night-night, Mummy," he said.

As Alfie sat up and rubbed his head, he caught sight of Mr Danson's shipwreck and a small plastic periscope breaking the surface of the water.

"ACTION STATIONS!" he shouted. "ENEMY SUBMARINE!"

"Roger that," said Grandpa. He laced his fingers together, held out his hands and shouted, "PREPARE TO LAUNCH DEPTH CHARGES!"

Grandma dropped her shovel, put one foot in his hands and grabbed hold of his shoulders.

"Ready?" said Grandpa. "One ... two ... three ... LAUNCH!"

As Grandpa jerked his hands up, Grandma shot into the air, performed a backward somersault and landed in the water with a huge splash.

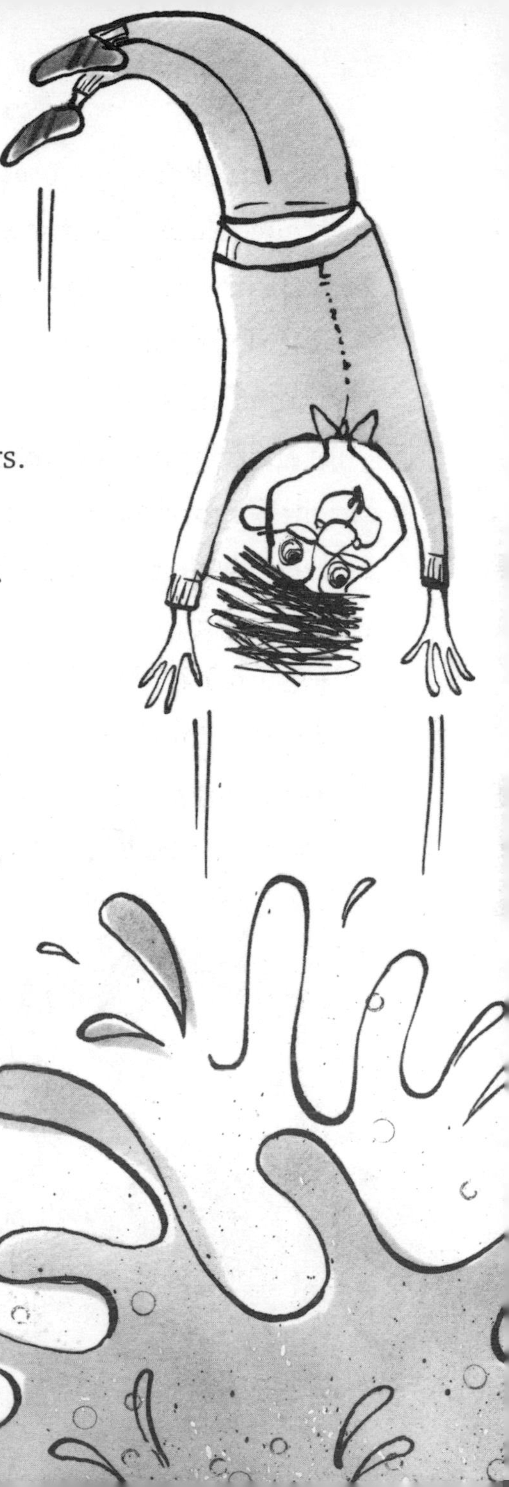

"RANGE TOO FAR!" shouted Alfie. "PREPARE NUMBER TWO!"

"Prepare number two!" shouted Grandpa as Mrs Jenkins scurried over and placed her foot into Alfie's hands.

"Ready?" said Alfie. "One ... two ... three ... LAUNCH!"

Mrs Jenkins took off like a scalded cat, hugging her knees to her chest before landing heavily on top of the periscope.

Seconds later she bobbed to the surface followed by Ricky, Wayne and Basbo, their masks hanging off and bits of broken wood floating all around them.

"DIRECT HIT!" reported Alfie. "Enemy submarine destroyed!"

"BULL'S-EYE!" yelled the crowd, throwing their hats in the air while generally agreeing that this was the best boat race ever.

"What happened, Mummy?" asked Twig as he woke up drenched in water. "Am I late for school?"

"No," said Hooey, handing him a shovel, "but Grandpa's lost his engines and if you want a pirate party you're going to have to paddle like you've never paddled before!"

"Gotcha!" said Twig. Hooey grabbed the other shovel while Will kicked his feet in the water at the back of the boat. Following

Grandpa and Alfie's orders, they quickly overtook the firemen and were neck and neck with the WI with just twenty metres to go.

"KEEP PADDLING!" shouted Hooey breathlessly. "We can take 'em! We can whup the WI!"

With the finishing line less than fifteen metres away, Hooey felt a rush of excitement; victory was within their grasp. If they could just keep it up for the last few metres...

Without warning, the boat swung around to the left. Hooey paddled faster, but that only made things worse. He looked up to see that Twig had dropped his shovel and was staring open-mouthed at something behind them.

"COME ON, TWIG!" he shouted. "KEEP SHOVELLING!"

But Twig wasn't listening, and when Hooey turned to follow his gaze, he saw why.

Gliding majestically up the river was a tiny wooden pirate ship made from the curved planks of old beer barrels. A skull and crossbones fluttered from the top of the mast, and standing proudly at the wheel was a girl with hooped earrings and a silver cutlass in her hand.

"Samantha," whispered Twig, clasping his hands to his chest. *"Samantha, can it really be you?"* And he stood there beaming as Grandpa's ship veered off towards the glass boat of the WI.

"Ahoy Samantha!" he called as her boat drew alongside. "Do you want to come to my pirate party?"

"Out of my way, NUMPTY," said Samantha.

As Samantha's ship swept past them towards the finishing line, Hooey tried desperately to paddle backwards. But it was too late. With a shattering of jam jars, they rammed into the WI and Hooey found himself splashing around in the river with Will, Twig, Grandpa, Alfie Rossiter and the ladies from the Women's Institute.

"Don't worry, everyone," Gladys called cheerfully, holding up some soggy lumps of wool. "I've knitted enough life jackets for all of us!"

PIRATE PARTY

Will stood on the bank clutching his soaking wet plans.

"I think," he said, "that I might have miscalculated the angle by a degree or two."

"Ah well," said Twig, wringing out his shorts. "You live and learn. Although I don't think I've learned anything since November. Or was it October?"

"Look," said Hooey, "they're going to present Samantha with her prize." Seeing the disappointment on Twig's face, he added, "Sorry about your party, Twig. Maybe next year, eh?"

* * *

The crowd was gathering expectantly, waiting for the mayor's announcement. Grandpa and Alfie were trying on waistcoats crocheted by the ladies from the WI, Bob the Baker was selling his new range of "Water Doughnuts" for half-price and Grandma was telling Mr Danson how they'd blown up an enemy submarine.

"I've given the crew some **Maritime Marshmallows** to keep their spirits up," explained Grandma. She pointed to Basbo and his friends, who were arguing with one another on the bank. "I told them we'd be happy to depth-charge them again next year, but they didn't seem very keen."

She raised her hand and as Mrs Jenkins high-fived it, they both shouted "**DEPTH CHARGE!**" and giggled so much that they had to cross their legs and sit down.

"All right everyone," announced the mayor through his megaphone. "This is the moment you've been waiting for. Pray silence for the result of the

SHRIMPTON-ON-SEA HOME-MADE BOAT RACE.

Grandma and Mrs Jenkins stopped giggling.

Grandpa and Alfie stopped trying on waistcoats.

The crowd stopped talking and fell silent.

"AND THE WINNER IS..."

Samantha smiled smugly and stepped forward to claim her prize.

"... JAKEY FRINTON!"

"Huh?" said Samantha.

"Wake up, Jakey!" cried Frank and Freddie Frinton, pulling him off his Lilo. And as they led a dazed-looking Jakey up to receive his prize, Hooey realized that the Lilo must have caught on the front of Samantha's boat so that she had accidentally pushed him all the way to the finishing line.

"Congratulations young man," said the mayor, shaking him by the hand. "Is there anything you'd like to say before I hand you your prize money?"

"Yeah, I guess so," said Jakey, running a hand through his tousled hair. "First of all, I'd like to thank the pretty pirate girl for helping me win." Here he winked at Samantha, who blushed and looked down at her shoes.

"And second, I want to thank the little magnetic dude who helped me find my keys."

whispered Twig.

"And if the pirate girl doesn't mind," continued Jakey, holding up the cheque, "I'd like to use half this money to hire her boat for the night, and the other half—" here he paused to look in Twig's direction— "to throw the best pirate party that Shrimpton-on-Sea has ever seen!"

Twig turned to Hooey with a look of disappointment on his face. "A private party?" he said. "That means we can't go, doesn't it?"

Hooey smiled. "I think, Twig, that what he actually said was **pirate party**."

Twig's eyes grew wider by the second. "A **pirate party**? You mean...?"

Hooey nodded.

"With swords and planks and puffy shirts and everything?"

"Almost certainly."

"But Hooey," said Twig, overcome with

emotion, "that's ... that's ... that's ..."

"Hang on a sec," said Hooey.

He walked over to the mayor and tapped him on the shoulder. "Excuse me," he said, "but could I borrow that for a moment?"

"Be my guest," said the mayor.

Hooey walked back to Twig and patted him on the arm. "OK, Twig," he said. "Whenever you're ready, just take a deep breath and go for it."

"That's ... that's ... that's ..."

Hooey held the megaphone up to Twig's mouth and pressed ON.

...SHER-WEET!

HOOEY HIGGINS and the Shark

STEVE VOAKE

Like sharks? Like pants? Like to see a shark IN pants?
Read this book and you ... Might!

READ THESE BOOKS -
THEY'RE NEARLY AS GOOD
AS PLAYING ON THAT Wii THINGY!